Shifty Business

Greg Trine

Art by Frank W. Dormer

Harcourt Children's Books
Houghton Mifflin Harcourt
Boston New York

Harcourt Children's Books is an imprint of Houghton Mifflin Harcourt Publishing Company.
www.hmhbooks.com

Text set in Adobe Garamond

Library of Congress Cataloging-in-Publication Data
Trine, Greg.
Shifty business / Greg Trine ; art by Frank W. Dormer.
pages cm. —(The adventures of Jo Schmo)
Summary: "Fourth-grade superhero Jo Schmo discovers a very unusual talent for shape-shifting as she and her dog Raymond try to stop a crime wave in San Francisco. Monsters and sharks and bad guys, oh my!"—Provided by publisher.
ISBN 978-0-547-80796-6 (hardback)
[1. Superheroes—Fiction. 2. Shapeshifting—Fiction. 3. Dogs—Fiction. 4. Humorous stories.] I. Dormer, Frank W., illustrator. II. Title.
PZ7.T7356Shi 2013
[Fic]—dc23
2013003915

Manufactured in the United States of America
DOC 10 9 8 7 6 5 4 3 2 1
4500415447

For Cruz—G.T.
For Grandpa Dormer—F.D.

contents

1

The Crime Tsunami

Superhero Jo Schmo didn't know that a crime tsunami was about to hit San Francisco. She didn't know about the crime wave, which is how all crime tsunamis begin. She didn't even know about the crime ripple, which is what you get before a crime wave. Ripple, wave, tsunami—that's the way it works in the crime world.

It had been years since a crime tsunami had hit San Francisco, so they were due for one. In fact, they were overdue. But Jo didn't know any of this.

She was too busy thinking about Kevin, Mitch, and David. Every superhero had a weakness or two. Jo Schmo had three.

Kevin had the best hair in class.

Mitch looked spectacular in green.

And David had exactly seventeen freckles that she absolutely adored.

So Jo was distracted . . . by her weaknesses. She could feel her strength draining away. She was pretty sure she couldn't stop a train in this condition. She probably couldn't even stop a bus—or a tricycle.

And that's when her phone buzzed in her desk. "A text message from Grandpa," Jo said to herself. Her grandfather was a retired sheriff who listened to his police radio day and night. When a crime was committed, he contacted Jo.

Car thieves in Chinatown. Go get 'em, Jo.

Jo would be happy to go get them. Only right

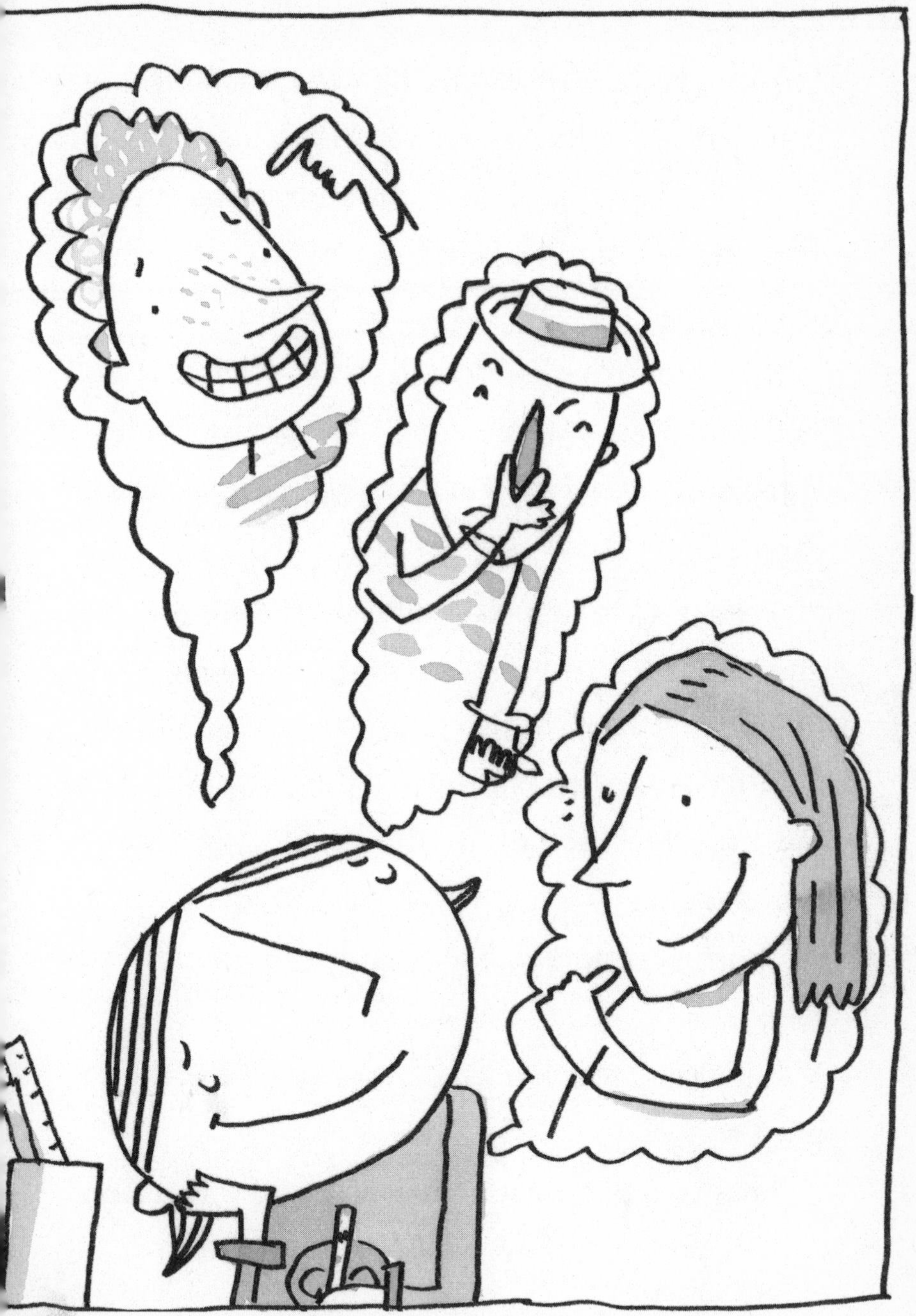

now she was a little low in the strength and energy department, thanks to Kevin, Mitch, and David.

Jo raised a weak hand. "Can I use the bathroom, Mrs. Freep?" she squeaked.

"Go get 'em, Jo," Mrs. Freep said under her breath so no one else could hear. What she said out loud was, "Absolutely." One of her students was a superhero, and that was just fine with Mrs. Freep.

So Jo, still feeling weak, stood up from her desk and dragged herself to the classroom door. Once outside the school, her strength returned and she sprinted across the blacktop to the bike rack where her trusty Schmomobile, and her dog, Raymond, were waiting.

"Ready to go catch bad guys, Raymond?" Jo asked.

Raymond gave her a look that said, "Lady, I was born ready."

That was good enough for Jo. She wasn't born

ready. She became a superhero when she inherited the cape.

She fired up the Schmomobile, and soon she and Raymond were racing down the sidewalk toward Chinatown. They arrived just in the elbow of time, which is sort of like arriving just in the neck of time. But elbow sounds way more interesting.

Wait a minute—it's nick of time, not neck of time. Never mind.

Up ahead she saw what looked like a couple of car thieves coming her way. How could she tell they were car thieves? Because they were traveling sixty miles per hour in a thirty-five-mile-per-hour zone. And they were on the sidewalk!

Raymond shot them a look that said, "This sidewalk ain't big enough for the two of us." Actually, there were three of them—four, if you count Jo. But you get the idea. The point is that Jo and Raymond were making a stand, and the bad guys better get off the sidewalk, or else!

The car thieves sped toward her.

"I stopped a train, Raymond. I can stop a car."

Raymond gave her a look that said, "If you say so, but if you don't mind, I think I'll stand over here." He stepped off the sidewalk onto the street.

Jo *had* stopped a train. The *Superhero Instruction Manual,* which she inherited along with the cape, had said stopping a speeding locomotive was all in the wrist. Was stopping a speeding car the same?

She hoped so. She put her hands out in front of her, making sure her wrists were placed just so. "I stopped a train," she kept telling herself. "I stopped a train. This has to work." The car kept coming, picking up speed.

Just before it hit, Jo closed her eyes.

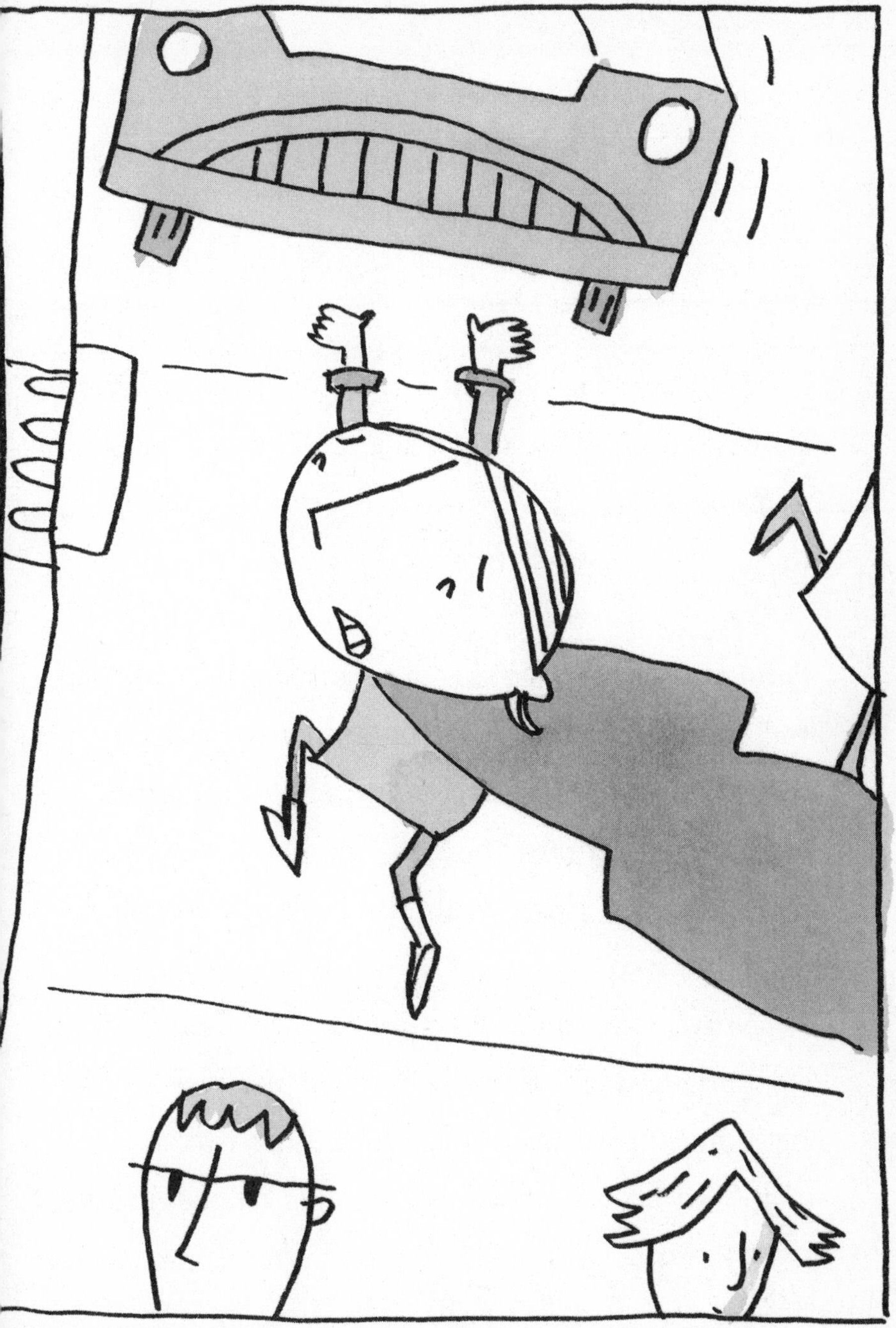

2

Numb Skull's Evil Plan

And before you could say "Jo Schmo stopped the speeding car and a couple of car thieves," Jo Schmo stopped the speeding car and a couple of car thieves. Then she used her famous Knuckle Sandwich on them and hung around until the police arrived.

"Wow," she said. "Stopping a car is exactly like stopping a train. It really is all in the wrist." She held out her hand, and Raymond high-fived it.

Jo had no idea that this was just the beginning

of the crime tsunami getting ready to hit San Francisco. But she was about to find out.

Three days earlier, there had been a Bad Guy and Evil Villain meeting in the abandoned warehouse district, where Numb Skull presided. Numb Skull was a retired boxer turned bad guy. He used to be a good guy, or at least an okay guy, but every time he was smacked in the head in the boxing ring, he lost a little of his good-guyness and his okay-guyness, until there was nothing left to do but pursue a life of crime. Which he did.

And now, Numb Skull ruled the abandoned warehouse district in San Francisco, where most of the bad guys lived. He had called the Bad Guy and Evil Villain meeting to get the crime tsunami rolling. As you know, waves roll, and tsunami waves roll rather hugely. And a huge wave would keep a superhero very busy.

This was Numb Skull's plan. If he could keep

Jo Schmo busy chasing other villains, he would be left alone to do his evil deeds. And he had plenty of evil deeds up his sleeve—even when he was wearing a tank top.

But back to the meeting . . .

"Ladies and gentlemen," Numb Skull began, "as you know, we have a pesky superhero in town named Jo Schmo. She might beat some of us, but she can't beat all of us."

Just the mention of Jo Schmo caused some in the crowd to shiver.

Others growled.

Numb Skull shook an angry fist in the air. He really hated fourth grade superheroes.

He explained how a crime tsunami worked. Overwhelm the crime fighter; that was the basic idea. And the crime fighter in question was none other than Jo Schmo.

"All in favor?" Numb Skull asked.

Everyone cheered. It was unanimous: everyone

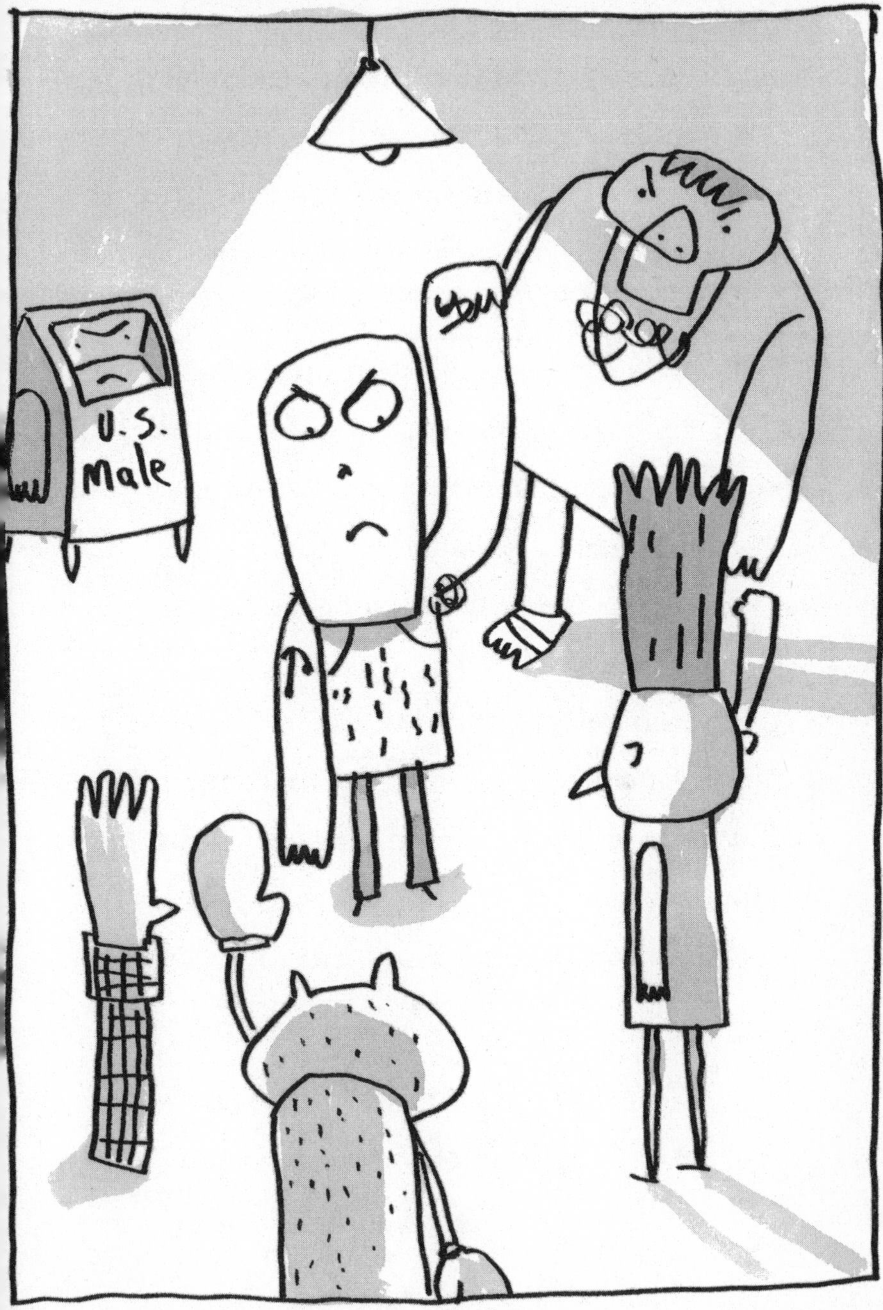
U.S.
Male

loved the idea of a crime tsunami. And it all began with a couple of car thieves in Chinatown.

Jo Schmo didn't know any of this. After she stopped the speeding car on the sidewalk, she headed back to class.

"That was the longest bathroom break in U.S. history," one of her classmates complained. This is true. But there had been three bathroom breaks that were longer in Canadian history and one that was *way* longer in the history of France.*

Jo didn't hear what her classmate was saying. She was too busy staring at Kevin's hair, Mitch in his green shirt, and David's seventeen adorable freckles. Once again, she could feel her strength slipping away.

"I love my weaknesses," she said to herself.

---

* Canada and France are into long bathroom breaks for some reason. Don't ask.

Shape-Shifting 101

When Jo got home from school, she headed straight for the shack in the backyard where her grandfather lived. She banged on the door and yelled, "Grandpa, it's Jo."

"Joe?"

"No, Jo."

"Oh, *Jo*. Come in, Jo. I thought I was talking to myself for a second there." Grandpa Joe still had his ear to the police radio, listening for more crimes. He turned down the volume and waited to hear about his granddaughter's latest adventure.

"Guess what, Gramps?" Jo said as she went inside.

"What?" Grandpa Joe asked, raising a bushy eyebrow. Then he raised the other one just to even things out. He hated having lopsided eyebrows.

"You know how stopping a speeding locomotive is all in the wrist?"

"Yeah?"

"You can stop a speeding car the same way."

"You don't say."

"I do say," Jo said.

Grandpa Joe gave her a high-five. "You can fly, you can stop a train, *and* you know how to stop a speeding car. Not bad, Jo. What's next?"

"Don't forget my famous Knuckle Sandwich." Jo had one of the best Knuckle Sandwiches the world has ever known. That, along with her Russian Toe Hold and Siberian Ear Tweak, made for one scary superhero.

"What's next?" Grandpa Joe said again. He hadn't forgotten about the Knuckle Sandwich; he just wanted to know what other superpowers Jo could come up with.

What's next? Good question, thought Jo. She hadn't thought much about it, not really. She was just happy to have stopped a speeding car. What kind of powers could she add to flying and stopping a speeding anything? Jo looked at her grandfather, who was still waiting for an answer. Seconds passed—then minutes. The clock on the wall ticked away. Outside a bird squawked.

And then, suddenly, it hit her. "Invisibility!" she said.

"Perfect," said Grandpa Joe. "You could get into the movies for free."

"No, wait a second." She had a better idea. And now, even her eyebrows shot up. "Not invisibility. Shape-shifting."

"Fabulous. You could turn yourself into a flea and get into the movies for free." Grandpa Joe was very big on getting into the movies for free.

"I could sneak around in the abandoned warehouse district, and no one would know I was there." Getting into the movies for free was all fine and dandy, but she was a superhero. Shape-shifting would come in handy for a superhero. The question was how to do it. "Where's the *Superhero*

Instruction Manual, Gramps?"

Grandpa Joe pulled the book off a shelf and opened it for a look. "Here it is. Shape-shifting, chapter nine." He turned to chapter nine and read it to himself. "Hmm," he said after a while.

Jo hated "Hmms." Especially her grandpa's. "Hmms" in general meant something wasn't quite right. And her grandpa's "Hmms" were the worst.

"What is it, Gramps?" Jo asked.

"It says that shape-shifting is all about thinking the right sort of shifting thoughts."

"Hmm . . ." Jo said. Even though she hated "Hmms," she couldn't help herself. Sometimes there was nothing else to say but "Hmm." She thought about the day she tried to learn to fly by thinking lofty thoughts. It wasn't easy. Now she had to think shape-shifting thoughts?

"What's a shape-shifting thought?" Jo asked.

"I suppose you just think about what you want to change into," her grandpa said. "Want to give it a go, Jo? Try shifting into a dog. Raymond needs a pal."

"Better a dog than a flea," Jo said. She thought of herself with a tail and furry paws. She let her tongue flop out of her mouth and threw in a few dog-size pants. Nothing happened. She was just a girl with her tongue hanging out.

"Think harder," Grandpa Joe said.

Jo thought harder. She scratched herself like a dog. She wagged her behind, even though she didn't have a tail. She waited for the moon to rise, and went outside and howled at it. Raymond walked over and gave her a look that said, "You're speaking my lingo."

Jo howled again. Raymond joined in. It was nice to have someone to howl at the moon with. They howled together, in two-part dog harmony.

But it was no use. Jo looked down at her hands, then she checked for a tail. Nothing had changed— nothing shifted. She was still one hundred percent Jo Schmo.

DYNO-Mike

While Jo Schmo was howling at the moon and not changing into a dog, Numb Skull was busy getting ready to commit the crime of the century. Or at least the crime of the week. The point is that it was a crime, and it was *his* crime, and that was all that mattered.

What was this crime, you ask? By the way, thanks for asking. Numb Skull's crime involved priceless jewels and gazillionaires and expensive cruise ships. But to make his plan work perfectly,

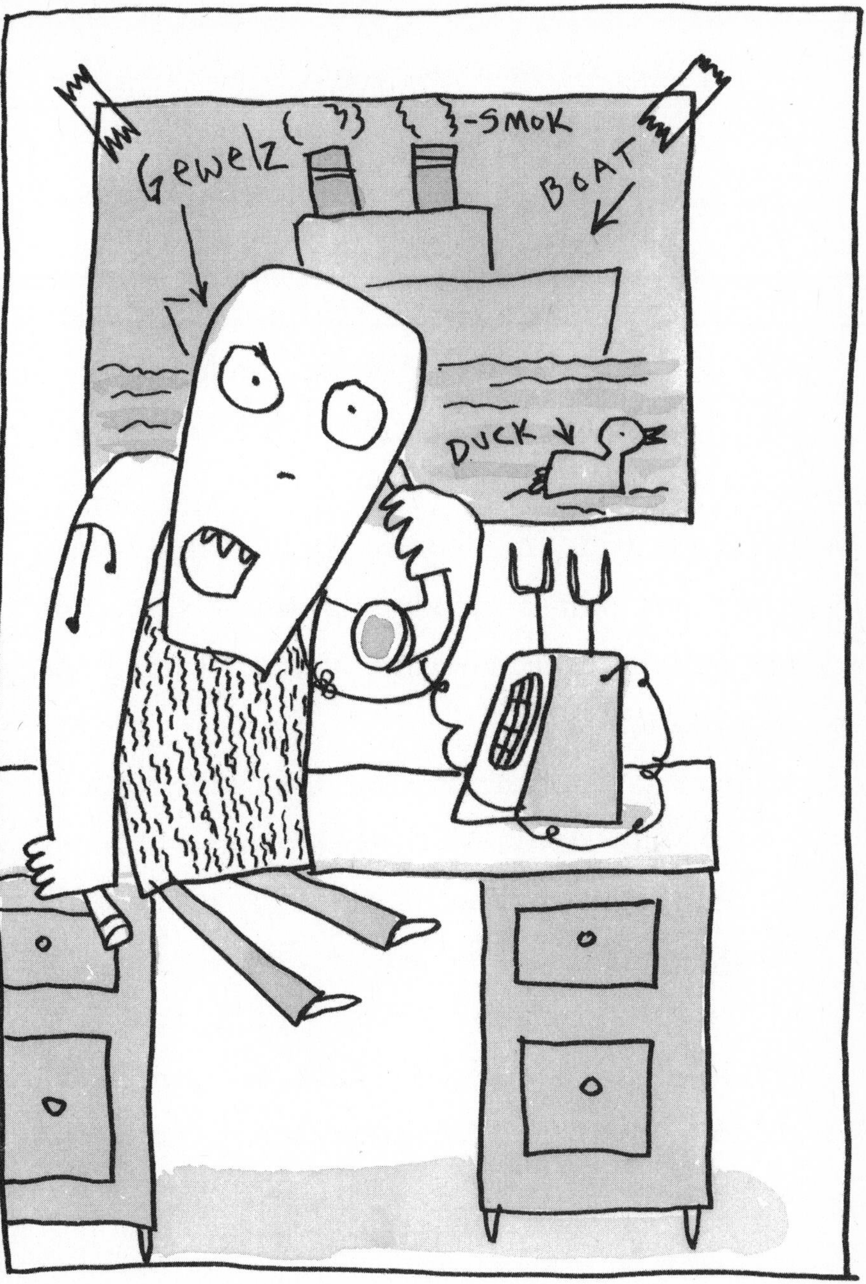
Gewelz
-SMOK
BOAT
DUCK

he needed a partner who could blow things up. And he knew just who to call.

Numb Skull picked up the phone and dialed his good friend from his days in Bad Guy School, Dyno-Mike, not to be confused with Firecracker Fred or Kaboom Karl. Fred or Karl would be Numb Skull's second choice, but they weren't exactly on speaking terms.

"Dyno-Mike, it's Numb Skull." Numb Skull could hear things exploding on the other end of the line. It made it very difficult to carry on a conversation.

"How'd you like to blow up a cruise ship?" Numb Skull yelled. "What's that? Yes, water is wet . . . Yes, the sky is blue . . . Of course ice cream is tasty." Numb Skull smiled. He didn't even have to talk Dyno-Mike into it. Something needed to be blown up, and Mike would be happy to do the job. "Meet me at my place in the abandoned warehouse district."

Numb Skull hung up the phone and turned to his good friend Harry Knuckles. Numb Skull and Harry had been friends even before their days in Bad Guy School. Like Numb Skull, Harry was also a retired boxer who had turned evil after being smacked in the head one too many times. Actually, it was a thousand too many times, but who's counting?

"Dyno-Mike is in," Numb Skull said.

"Great. What's the plan?" Harry Knuckles cracked his knuckles, which were, of course, hairy, and listened while Numb Skull explained his evil plan.

The plan was all about sinking a cruise ship full of gazillionaires and stealing their priceless jewels. This was all well and good, as far as Harry Knuckles was concerned. But two things bothered him. One, how would they get the jewels from a ship that was at the bottom of the San Francisco Bay? Two, would he be able to punch anyone?

Harry Knuckles was a retired boxer. He hadn't punched someone in a very long time. He didn't want to forget how.

"Not to worry," Numb Skull said. "There will be plenty of security guards to punch."

"But how will we get the jewels from a sunken ship?"

And right then Numb Skull almost let out his famous evil laugh. As laughs go, Numb Skull had a good one, but he decided to wait until the plot thickened a bit more. Instead, he dragged Harry into his garage to show him more of his evil plan.

"What is it?" Harry didn't know what he was staring at. It looked like a metal hot dog that was as big as a car.

"It's my own personal submarine," Numb Skull said proudly. "Turbocharged and everything. Zero to fifty in sixty-four seconds. Dyno-Mike will sink the ship, then we'll swoop in and steal the jewels, and—"

"We'll be rich beyond our wildest dreams?" Harry said.

"Pretty much." Just then, Numb Skull didn't care about waiting until the plot thickened. He could feel his evil laugh climbing up his throat, wanting air. And so he tilted his head back and let it out.

"Mwah-ha-ha!"

Boy, that felt good.

5

unSweet Dreams

Jo Schmo was pretty upset that she couldn't shape-shift into a dog. She howled at the moon until she was hoarse. Then she howled some more. But nothing happened.

Later, as she was changing into her green pajamas, she looked down at Raymond and said, "I can't believe it, Raymond. I can't shape-shift at all."

Raymond shot her a look that said, "Yeah, but you're the second-best moon howler I've ever seen."

Jo got into bed and tied a string around her big toe. The string led out the window and down to her grandpa's shack. If any crimes were committed in the middle of the night, he would tug on the string to wake her up.

"Good night, Raymond," Jo said.

Raymond's look said, "Sweet dreams."

Jo had dreams that night, but they were anything but sweet. She dreamed that Frankenstein's monster was after Kevin, Mitch, and David, and she had to rescue them, which was not easy, since every time she got close to the three boys, she felt weak. But in a dream anything can happen. She used her Knuckle Sandwich, then the Siberian Ear Tweak, and was just about to finish off the beast with the Russian Toe Hold, when he beat her to it. He grabbed her toe and began tugging. *Tug, tug, tug. Tug, tug, tug.*

"Ow, ow, ow," Jo said.

Then she woke up and noticed that the string

attached to her toe was doing the tugging. "It was all a dream," she said to herself as she untied the string. At least Kevin, Mitch, and David were safe. "Raymond, wake up. Time to go catch bad guys."

Raymond opened a tired eye and . . . yelped! He opened his other eye and double yelped as he backed away from Jo. He gave her a look that said, "Either you're not Jo Schmo or someone whacked you with the ugly stick."

Jo went to her closet mirror for a look, and—

Yelped! What she saw was not Jo Schmo at all. While she slept she had shape-shifted into Frankenstein's monster, scars and all. She even had bolts in her neck. But she also had great hair. She had seventeen adorable freckles. And she had on her green pajama top that looked, well . . . spectacular.

Jo looked at Raymond, who was still cowering in the corner of the bedroom. "It's me, Raymond. I shape-shifted. Let's go show Grandpa."

Raymond gave her a look that said, "Who are you and what have you done with Jo Schmo?" Then he shot her another look. "By the way, nice hair."

"It's me, Raymond," Jo said again. "Let's go."

Raymond followed Jo downstairs and out into the backyard. It sounded like the Jo he knew and loved, but he wasn't sure.

"Grandpa, it's—"

This is as far as she got. One look at the thing

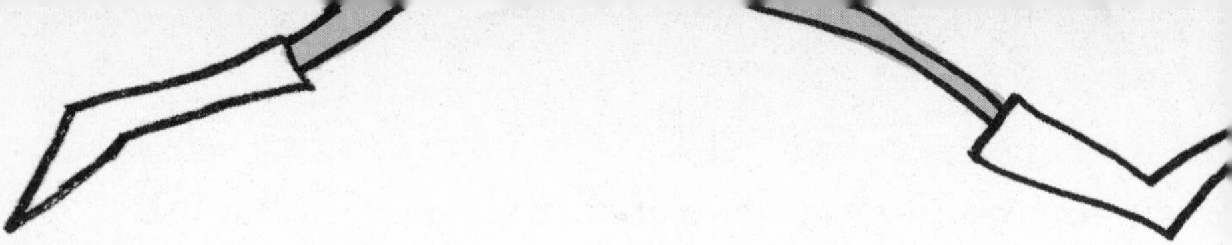

coming in the door and Grandpa yelped like . . .
Raymond. He backed himself into a corner and
held his police radio up for protection.

"Grandpa, it's Jo. I shape-shifted while I was
sleeping."

Grandpa Joe looked at Raymond for con-
firmation.

Raymond gave him a look that said, "It sure
sounds like her."

"Can you change back?" he said. "I mean, it
looks like you've been hit with the ugly stick."

"I don't know," Jo said. "Maybe I should stay
like this for a while. A superhero that looks like
this is a very scary thing."

"Good point." Grandpa Joe put the police radio
down. "There's a lot going on. Bank robbers, bar
fights, drug deals, jewel thieves, terrorist plots,
purse snatchers, home robberies, store break-ins,

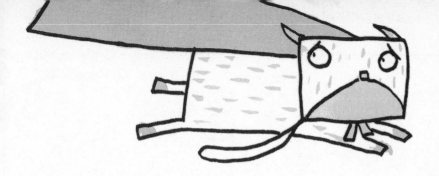

car thieves. This is more than a crime wave, Jo.
It's—"

"A crime tsunami?"

"Exactly," Grandpa Joe said. "Go get 'em, Jo.
Who are you going after first?"

"That's the great thing about crime tsunamis,
Gramps," Jo said as she and Raymond headed for
the door. "I can take my pick."

Once outside, Jo and Raymond sprinted across
the backyard and climbed onto the Schmomobile.

A superhero who looked like Frankenstein's
monster was a scary thing. A superhero who looked
like that while speeding down the sidewalk at sixty
miles an hour was even scarier.

ThE BaD GUYS (GirlS)

You might think that all bad guys are guys. Hence the phrase "bad guys." This is not always true. It just sounds better than saying "bad guys and girls" and way better than saying "bad persons." The fact is that some of the world's most famous bad guys were, well, not exactly guys. Ever hear of Cruella de Vil, Ursula the Sea Witch, Betty Sludgefoot?

During the Bad Guy and Evil Villain meeting in the abandoned warehouse district, as Numb Skull explained the details of how to create a crime tsunami, two girls sitting in the back were getting ideas. Their names were Zoey and Claire, and both of them were big fans of Cruella de Vil and Ursula the Sea Witch. They had no idea who Betty Sludgefoot was, but two out of three isn't bad.

"I've never been part of a crime tsunami before," Zoey said.

"Me neither," Claire said.

After the meeting, the two girls walked along the waterfront discussing what kind of crime to commit.

"How about a late-night shopping spree?" Claire asked.

Zoey put her hands on her hips. "What kind of crime is that?"

"Depends on how late we go. All the stores will be closed. We break in and take what we want. We'll have the place to ourselves."

"Good point," Zoey said. She despised shopping when it was crowded. She even hated Black Friday.

"Come to think of it, I could use a new pair of jeans and some shoes."

"Uh-huh," Claire said. "And we'll probably have to steal a car so we'll have a way to get around."

"And maybe rob a bank while we're at it so we'll have money to go on vacation with all our new clothes."

"Bermuda," Claire suggested.

"Or Mexico."

"Someplace with a beach."

"Exactly."

The two girls slapped a high-five, then they knuckle-bumped. "I like how we think," said Claire.

"So do I." Zoey had gotten a D in thinking at school, but that was then . . . this was now.

Later that night Zoey and Claire crept out of the warehouse district, heading for the shopping district and the stealing-cars district. There wasn't really a stealing-cars district. Anyplace would do. All you needed were cars and people willing to do the crime. But you get the idea.

Zoey and Claire were willing. They really wanted new jeans and shoes—and a vacation. And they needed a car to make it happen.

"How about that one?" Claire said, pointing.

"Perfect," Zoey said, reaching for her lock-picking tools.

Minutes later they were driving down the street. Zoey was very tempted to let out her evil laugh, but she thought she'd wait until the plot thickened a little more. After all, stealing a car was just phase one in their evil plan. They still had much to do.

Fortunately, the night was still young. There was plenty of time to steal the clothes, rob a bank, and go on vacation.

7

The Last National Bank

Raymond had on his cape, which meant that as the Schmomobile raced toward downtown San Francisco, he drooled like no dog had ever drooled. He was a super dog and he was full of super drool. It made sense.

Raymond looked up at Jo. "Where to, boss?" his look said.

"Keep an eye peeled, Raymond. The first bad guy we come to gets it."

So began a night of catching bad guys. Talk about

a crime tsunami. Bar fighters and purse snatchers, car thieves and terrorists. Jo Schmo got the best of them using her famous Knuckle Sandwich, and now and then the Siberian Ear Tweak and the Russian Toe Hold. Raymond watched from the sidelines and drooled a lot, thinking of pork chops and other tasty dog treats, which made him drool even more.

Innocent bystanders were shocked to see Frankenstein's monster fighting crime. The bad guys were even more shocked.

"Yikes!" screamed a car thief.

"Aaugh!" yelled a purse snatcher.

"Let go of my toe!" cried a terrorist.

It was a very busy night.

By the time they caught up with Zoey and Claire, the two girls had already broken into several clothing stores and were now wearing brand-new jeans and shoes. They were also coming out of the Last National Bank of San Francisco, holding bags of cash. All they needed now was a vacation involving a beach, and their evil plan would be complete.

But not if Jo Schmo could help it. She and Raymond were racing up in the Schmomobile.

"Those two look guilty," Raymond's look said. He had an eye for guilty-looking people, especially ones who were coming out of the Last National

Bank of San Francisco in the middle of the night, holding bags of cash. These two looked guilty all right—call it dog's intuition.

"Halt in the name of—" Jo yelled, skidding to a stop.

Halt in the name of what? This was the hardest part of superhero work. Jo Schmo never knew what to add after "Halt in the name of." Halt in the name of fourth grade superheroes? Halt in the name of my Knuckle Sandwich? Halt out of the goodness of your heart?

While Jo was trying to think of the proper ending to "Halt in the name of," the bank robbers sped away in their stolen vehicle, and Raymond gave her a look that said, "You did it again, boss."

"Halt because I said so!" she yelled finally.

But it was too late. Zoey and Claire were long gone. Or shortly gone. The point is that they were nowhere in sight.

Jo hopped back on the Schmomobile and raced after them. She had a hunch where they might be headed. They were bad guys—the girl variety of bad guys—and they had to go someplace to count the loot, which is what you did after robbing a bank. And what better place to count loot than—

"The abandoned warehouse district?" said Raymond's look.

"That's my guess," Jo said. She headed toward the abandoned warehouse district, steering with her elbows so she could crack her knuckles. She had to get ready. "Knuckle Sandwich, coming right up."

Not to mention the Siberian Ear Tweak and the Russian Toe Hold.

Monster Chase

Renowned newspaperman Jasper "Scoop" Johnson sat in Margie's Diner at the edge of the abandoned warehouse district, pencil in hand, waiting for his next big story. He had no idea that a crime tsunami was starting up, but he was keeping his eyes peeled. And his ears peeled, for that matter. He was also peeling a banana, which wasn't an easy thing to do while holding a pencil. But if anyone could do it, Jasper "Scoop" Johnson could. He could also chew gum and walk at the same time.

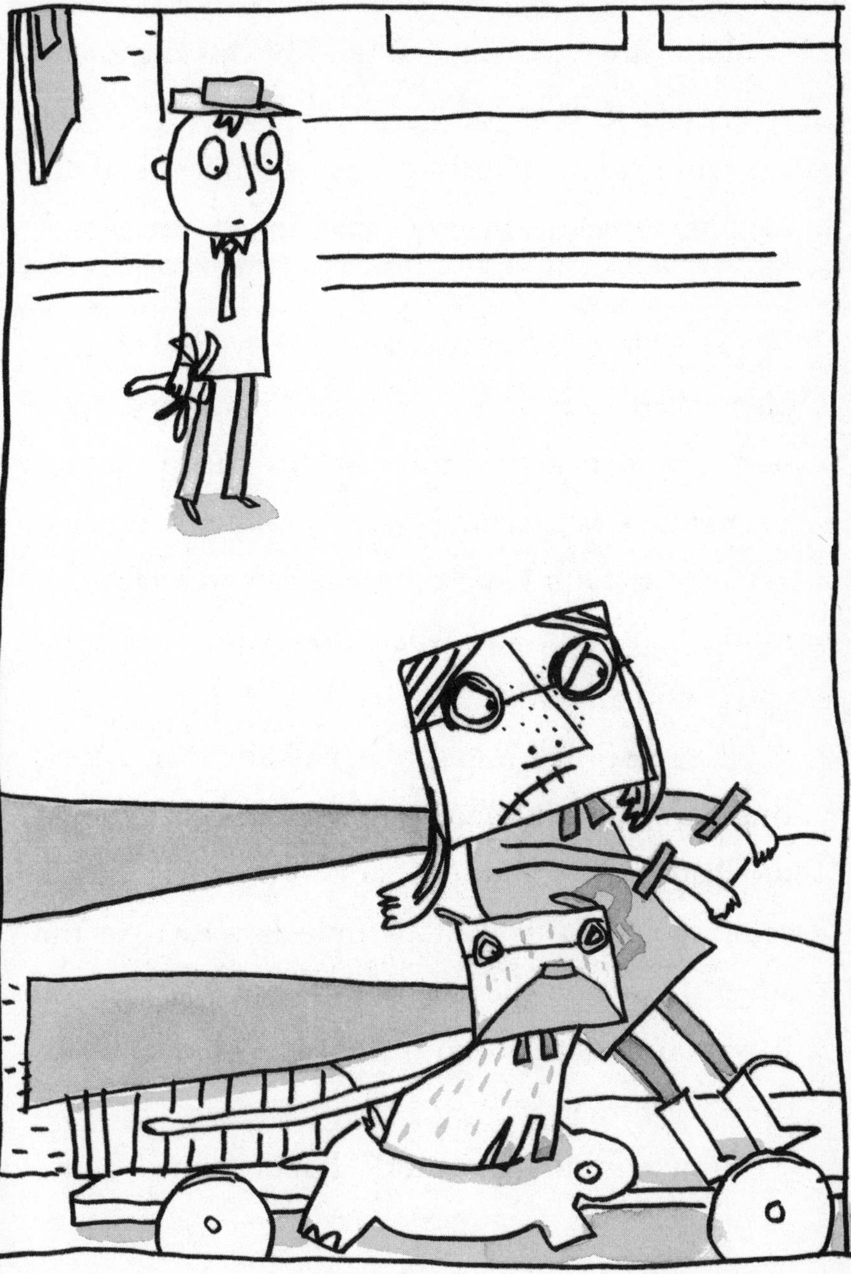

He finished his banana, paid for his meal, and stepped outside into the night air. And that's when a car zoomed by at nearly a hundred miles per hour, heading straight for the abandoned warehouse district.

"That's a getaway vehicle if I've ever seen one," Jasper said. And let's face it, as a newspaperman, he'd seen plenty. His senses were trained to notice such things as speeding getaway vehicles, because where you found speeding getaway vehicles you found bad guys, and where you found bad guys you found a story.

Jasper "Scoop" Johnson was all about the story. But before he could hop in his car and chase down the bad guys—and the story—another vehicle came racing his way. This time it wasn't on the street. It was on the sidewalk, and it wasn't a car. It was some sort of motorized skateboard, driven by—

"Frankenstein's monster!" Jasper yelped as he

dove back into the doorway of Margie's Diner. The speeding monster zoomed by, accompanied by a dog that was drooling way more than any dog should ever drool.

"A monster riding a motorized skateboard, chasing a getaway vehicle. What a scoop!" Jasper said, stepping back onto the sidewalk. He hopped into his car and gave chase.

Halfway down the block he had a frightening thought. He was chasing a monster.

While Jasper was busy *chasing* a monster, two girls who had just robbed a bank and a few clothing stores while dreaming of vacations involving a beach were trying to get *away* from a monster.

Not to mention a drooling dog.

Claire was in the driver's seat. Zoey rode shotgun, while calling out directions. "Turn right, make a left, speed up . . . Aaaah!"

Claire shot Zoey a look. "What's wrong?"

"Frankenstein's monster is after us. I forgot to yell earlier."

"Aaaah!" yelled Claire.

"What's wrong?"

"I forgot to yell earlier also."

But Frankenstein's monster, who was really a shape-shifted Jo Schmo, was nowhere to be seen. She and Raymond, who had just missed running over renowned newspaperman Jasper "Scoop" Johnson, were now roaming the streets of the abandoned warehouse district.

"See anything, Raymond?"

Raymond shook his dog head and gave her a look that said, "Nope, but I think we're being followed."

9

Jo Puts Two and Two Together

Numb Skull's evil plan was working. The crime tsunami was in full swing, and it was keeping Jo Schmo out of his hair, at least for now. And so when Dyno-Mike arrived, they got down to business, planning out the jewel heist of the century. Or at least of the week.

The plan was simple. Harry Knuckles would punch every guard he could find, Dyno-Mike would plant the explosives, the ship would sink, and then Numb Skull would swoop in with his own personal submarine and steal the jewels. You can't really swoop underwater, but you get the idea.

The point is that they were going to be—

"Rich beyond our wildest dreams," Harry Knuckles said.

Exactly.

But mapping out the plan wasn't good enough. Not for Dyno-Mike, anyway. He wanted to practice, do some sort of test run. And so while Jo Schmo was wandering around the abandoned warehouse district on the Schmomobile with Raymond in the sidecar, Numb Skull, Harry Knuckles, and Dyno-Mike were at the waterfront for exploding practice, which is a lot like blowing-things-up practice, or *kaboom* practice.

"Ready? Set? Go!" Numb Skull yelled.

Harry Knuckles fake-punched a couple of invisible guards. Dyno-Mike placed a small amount of explosives on a rowboat and shoved

it away from the dock. Numb Skull sat in his
submarine, ready to swoop in.

Seconds ticked by. "Wait for it, wait for it,"
whispered Dyno-Mike. Then—

Kaboom!

"Mwah-ha-ha!"

• • •

Raymond gave Jo a look that said, "Is it just me or did something just go *kaboom*?"

"I heard it," Jo said. "I also heard a *'Mwah-ha-ha,'* which means some evil person is celebrating something . . . evil."

With her keen mind, Jo began to put two and two together.

"Four?" Raymond's look said.

Jo shook her head. Something just blew up and someone was celebrating the blowing up. That's as far as her keen mind got, because right then her ears, which were also fairly keen, heard something.

"Counting," Raymond's look said. "Someone's counting—"

"The loot," Jo said. She brought the Schmo-mobile to a stop and locked it to a pole. Then she and Raymond raced along on foot, listening.

"Forty-seven, forty-eight, forty-nine . . ."

They stopped in front of a warehouse door.

"Fifty-four, fifty-five, fifty-six . . ."

Raymond gave Jo a look that said, "What's the plan, boss?"

"You stay here, Raymond. I'll go around back and chase them out the front."

Raymond didn't understand. He gave Jo one of those tilt-the-head-and-look-confused dog looks. She was going to chase the bad guys out the front? He didn't have a Knuckle Sandwich. He didn't have a Siberian Ear Tweak—or a Russian Toe Hold. He didn't even have hands. He was just a super dog who was full of super drool.

"Exactly," Jo said. "Pork chops, Raymond. Pizza, hot dogs, hamburgers." Then she ran around to the back of the building.

10

Dog Slobber

There were no lights in the alleyway behind the building, and Jo Schmo was afraid of the dark. She had to keep reminding herself that she was a superhero and she had the best Knuckle Sandwich the world has ever known. "I stopped a train," she whispered to herself. "I stopped a speeding car."

Saying this didn't help at all. An alleyway at night in the abandoned warehouse district was a very scary place.

"Ninety-five, ninety-six, ninety-seven . . ."

The bank robbers were still counting the loot. Jo found the back door and tried the knob. Locked. No problem if your name is Jo Schmo. She busted through the door with one punch and found herself in a dark hallway.

"One hundred seven, one hundred eight, one hundred nine . . ."

The bank robbers were too excited counting the loot to be bothered by other things—like the sound of a splintering back door. Or the sound of a superhero creeping down the hall. They had other things on their minds (besides the loot), like vacations involving a beach.

"I hope Raymond is still drooling," Jo whispered to herself.

Of course Raymond was still drooling. He had on his cape, which meant Drool City. And thanks to

Jo, he was also thinking of his favorite foods, like pork chops and pizza, which made him drool even more.

But Raymond was nervous. Any second Jo would be chasing the bank robbers out the front door, and how was he going to deal with that? So as he drooled, he practiced a dog version of the Knuckle Sandwich. Think Knuckle Sandwich with lots of fur. He also threw in a few canine kicks and swished his tail around like a whip.

But back to Jo Schmo . . .

At the end of the hall, there was a light on. This is where the counting was coming from. Jo cracked her knuckles and—

The counting stopped. They didn't hear Jo break down the back door, but they heard her crack her knuckles. Go figure.

"The jig is up," Jo said to herself. She stopped creeping down the hall and started running, which is what you do when the jig is up. The bank robbers knew she was coming; she didn't have time to creep.

By the time Jo reached the room with the light on, Zoey and Claire were headed out another door—the front door—where Raymond was waiting for them, practicing his dog Knuckle Sandwich, his canine kicks, and his tail swish.

Fortunately, he didn't need any of his newly acquired moves. The dog drool did the trick. When Zoey and Claire stepped on the drool, their feet came out from under them, and Jo finished them off with a couple of Knuckle Sandwiches.

"What a scoop!" said Jasper "Scoop" Johnson, who witnessed the event from across the street. He knew a good story when he saw one.

Frankenstein's monster?

In a cape?

With great boxing skills?

"Stop the press!" Jasper yelled.

He had always wanted to say that.

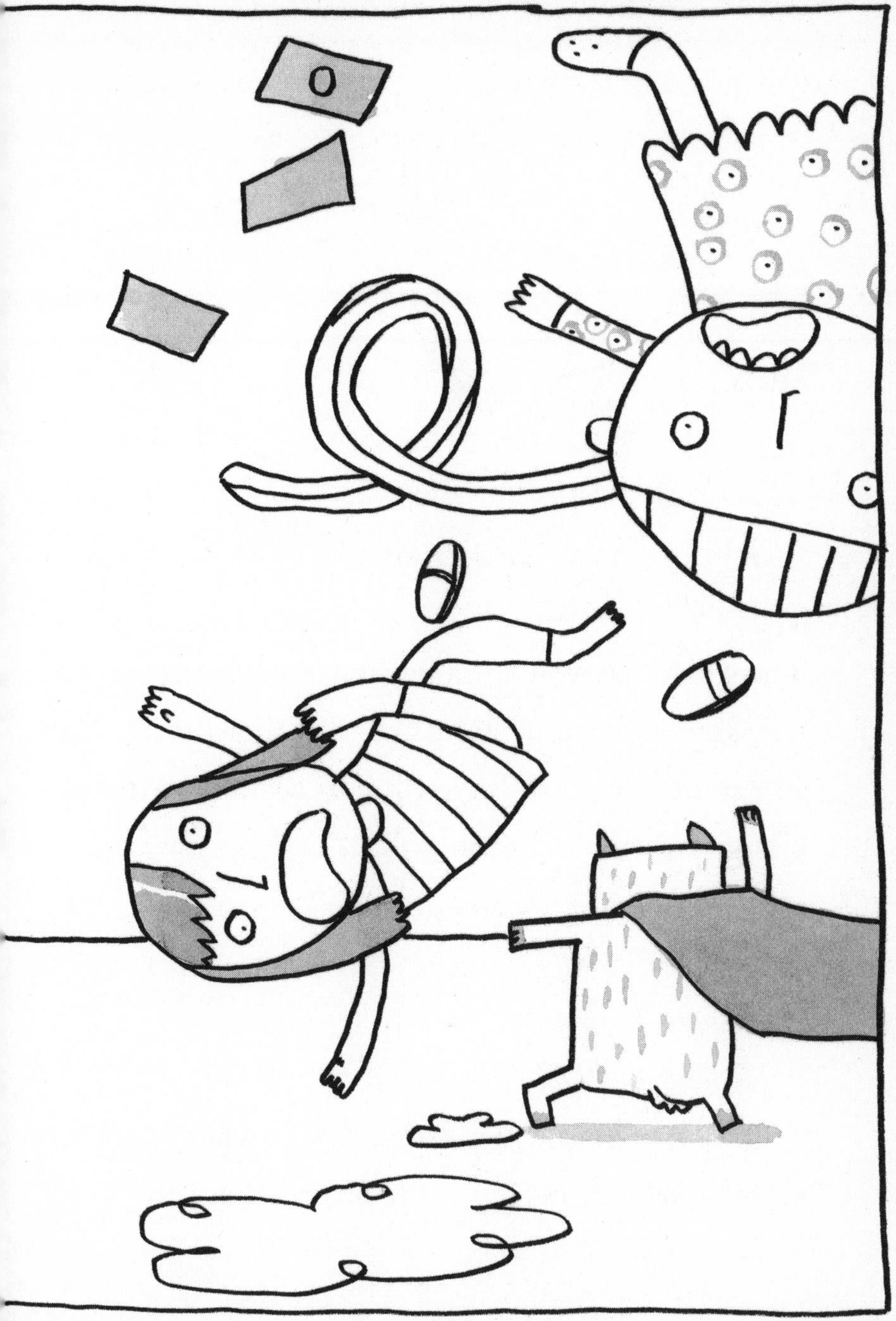

Triple Whammy

The police arrived to take Zoey and Claire off to jail, Jasper "Scoop" Johnson ran off to write his story, and Jo and Raymond were now cruising along on the Schmomobile, looking for more crime-tsunami participants.

"Mwah-ha-ha!"

"Mwah-ha-ha!"

"Mwah-ha-ha!"

Uh-oh, thought Jo Schmo. That's what you call a triple whammy. It meant an evil bad guy—or the girl variety of a bad guy—was celebrating three evil deeds. Or maybe three evil bad guys were celebrating one evil deed.

"Or it might be three evil bad guys celebrating three evil deeds," Raymond's look said.

The point is that something big and evil was going on right under their noses. "Keep your ears perked, Raymond," Jo said.

Raymond gave her a look that said, "I'm a dog. My ears are always perked."

"*Mwah-ha-ha!*"

"*Mwah-ha-ha!*"

"*Mwah-ha-ha!*"

"It's coming from the waterfront," Jo said. "Something smells fishy."

"Or course," Raymond's look said. "It's the waterfront. It's supposed to smell fishy." And right then, the thought of fish made him drool even more than usual.

"No, I don't mean that." With her keen mind,

Jo again began to put two and two together.

"Four?" Raymond's look said.

Jo shook her head. "One of the evil laughs was muffled, like it was trapped inside something. Some kind of confined space at the waterfront."

"A submarine?" Raymond's look said.

Talk about putting two and two together. Jo Schmo wasn't the only one with a keen mind.

"That's it." Jo gunned the Schmomobile. But by the time they reached the waterfront, the evil laughs had stopped, and there was no sign of a submarine.

Funny thing about submarines . . . sometimes they're underwater.

Jo and Raymond stopped the Schmomobile at the end of a pier and looked out over the bay. "See anything, Raymond?"

"Nope," Raymond's look said. He thought back to their last adventure, where he had to do an awful lot of dog-paddling. He sure hoped there wasn't an evil laugher in a submarine out there.

"It's late, Raymond," Jo said. "Let's go home."

They climbed onto the Schmomobile and headed back to Crimshaw Avenue.

The next morning Jo was back to normal. No bolts in the neck, no scars, no more seventeen adorable freckles. She was one hundred percent Jo Schmo.

She went to the backyard and gave her grandpa a report of the night before—Zoey and Claire, renowned newspaperman Jasper "Scoop" Johnson, an evil laugher inside a submarine. It had been a very busy night.

"Submarine?" Grandpa Joe's eyebrows shot straight up and stayed there. "That doesn't sound good."

"Tell me about it," Raymond's look said. "I hate dog-paddling."

"Better get to school," Grandpa Joe said. "I'll text you if anything happens."

Jo was exhausted from all the crime fighting the night before. During class, as Mrs. Freep was explaining a math problem involving Kate and how to divide four doughnuts between seven friends,

Jo began to nod off. Later, while Kim was giving her oral report on the Santa Barbara Mission, Jo fell fast asleep. She dreamed she was doing battle with a rat the size of a beagle, while everyone around her stood on top of desks and said things like "Eeek!" and "Yikes!" and "That's one big rat!"

When Jo opened her eyes, everyone in the class was saying "Eeek!" and "Yikes!" and "That's one big rat!"

And they were all pointing at Jo Schmo.

"Not again," Jo said to herself. "Don't tell me I shape-shifted in my sleep again." She looked down at her hands. Sure enough, they were rat paws. She looked behind her. Yep—she had a tail.

Mrs. Freep was standing on her desk yelling, "Jo Schmo, help us!" But, of course, Jo Schmo was the reason they needed help.

There was nothing for Jo to do but get out of there, which is exactly what she did. She raced out of the classroom as fast as her little rat feet could carry her. Then she sprinted across the playground to the bike rack, where the Schmomobile and Raymond were waiting.

Raymond gave the rat a look that said, "Want to arm-wrestle?"

"It's me, Raymond. It's Jo."

Raymond wasn't convinced. She looked an awful lot like a beagle-size rat.

Jo said, "We should come up with a code phrase so that when I shape-shift you'll know it's me."

"Code phrase?" Raymond's look said. "Okay, how about 'Raymond is the coolest dog ever.'"

"That'll work."

12

Ah-Choo!

The problem with being a beagle-size rat is that
Jo was too short to drive the Schmomobile. Plus,
she didn't have hands, which would have made it
very difficult, anyway. She and Raymond had to
walk home. If she had to shape-shift in her sleep
again, why couldn't it be into something useful,
like Frankenstein's monster?

"Tell me about it," Raymond's look said.

They walked and walked. "You know what
sounds good right now?" Jo asked. "A big hunk

of cheese." She stopped in front of Fast Freddie's Deli, where there were many big hunks of cheese, and took a deep breath. And when she did, she sneezed, and when she sneezed she shape-shifted back into Frankenstein's monster.

"Uh-oh," Raymond's look said. "The ugly stick is back."

"Never mind that," Jo said. "Let's go get the Schmomobile." She waggled her fingers. "I have hands, Raymond."

On the way back to school to get the

Schmomobile, Jo sneezed again and shape-shifted into a werewolf.

"Great," Raymond's look said. "A howl-at-the-moon buddy." Then he gave Jo a look that said, "Code phrase, please."

"Raymond is the coolest dog ever."

A few minutes later, Jo sneezed again and shape-shifted into Mrs. Freep. She almost felt like giving herself homework or coming up with impossible word problems. Obviously, things were getting out of control. She needed to talk to her grandpa, and she needed to talk to him now.

Grandpa Joe was surprised to see a strange lady knocking on his door. He recognized the drooling Raymond, but not Mrs. Freep.

"It's me, Grandpa. It's Jo."

"Shape-shifted in your sleep again?"

"No, I sneezed and shape-shifted."

Grandpa nodded and went to the bookshelf

for the *Superhero Instruction Manual*. He read the chapter on shape-shifting again. "Not much here, Jo. It just says it's all about thinking shape-shifting thoughts. It doesn't say anything about sneezing."

Jo stopped thinking up impossible word problems and gave Grandpa Joe her full attention. "I can't help what I think about when I sleep, Grandpa. And sometimes you just have to sneeze."

"The good news is that you can still fight crime as an old lady, Jo. You can still stop trains. You can still stop speeding cars." He shot her a look. "How's your Knuckle Sandwich?"

"Not sure. Put your face over here, Gramps."

Grandpa Joe leaned in.

Smack!

"Good as ever."

"You can say that again," Grandpa Joe said, rubbing his jaw.

The crime tsunami was still in full swing. This

meant that Jo didn't have to be woken up by a string tied around her toe. There were plenty of bad guys out there, even the girl variety. Jo decided to wait until late at night to go after them.

Meanwhile, she had dinner with her mom and grandpa. Mrs. Schmo was delighted to have Mrs. Freep over for dinner. She had no idea where her daughter was, but she enjoyed having an adult conversation for a change.

"How's Jo doing in school?" Mrs. Schmo asked.

"She's the best student I've ever had."

Later that night, Jo Schmo, who still looked like Mrs. Freep, and Raymond climbed onto the Schomomobile and sped toward the waterfront. Ever since she heard the triple-whammy evil laugh, one of them muffled as if it was coming from inside a submarine, Jo couldn't get the thought out of her head.

But just before they reached the water, Jo sneezed again and shape-shifted back into a werewolf. She brought the Schmomobile to a stop, looked up at the moon, and howled.

Raymond gave her a look that said, "I love you!"

13

Curses!

CRIME TSUNAMI CRESTS IN THE CITY

By Jasper "Scoop" Johnson

A long-overdue crime tsunami has hit the city of San Francisco, which has officials wondering, *Where is Jo Schmo when we need her?* At a time when crime is peaking, the diminutive catcher of bad guys is nowhere to be seen.

"Jo Schmo always seems to show up just when we need her," said police chief Wilson Dunbar. "But not this time." Schmo, who in the past has brought down such arch criminals as Dr. Dastardly and his evil assistant, Pete, seems to have vanished into thin air. But not to worry, ladies and gentlemen. It turns out that Miss Schmo is not the only show in town. There's a new crime fighter in these parts— and his name is Frankenstein's monster. Actually, this reporter doesn't know what his name is. But he's stepping up where Jo Schmo stepped down . . .

The article went on and on about Frankenstein's monster catching a couple of clothing store thieves/ bank robbers/dreamers of vacations involving a beach.

"Curses!" yelled Numb Skull, throwing down the newspaper. Just what he needed, a monster crime fighter. Numb Skull had always hated monsters, especially the kind that went after bad guys. Weren't monsters supposed to *be* the bad guys?

The test run of his evil plot had been a success.

Now it was just a matter of sinking the cruise ship, swooping in with his submarine, and stealing the jewels. But Numb Skull was worried. Reading about Frankenstein's monster sent a shiver down his spine.

Where was Jo Schmo when he needed her? he wondered. He'd much rather tangle with a diminutive fourth grade superhero than a monster with creepy scars and bolts in his neck.

As it turns out, Jo Schmo was not far away, only she didn't look at all like Jo Schmo. She didn't even look like Frankenstein's monster. She was a werewolf and was currently down by the waterfront, howling at the moon. Raymond joined in. Their two-part dog harmony was . . . above average.

"Okay, enough of that," Jo said. "Let's get to work."

"What's the plan?" Raymond's look said.

"Keep your ears perked, Raymond, especially for muffled evil laughs."

As you know, Raymond was a dog, and a dog's ears are always perked. They walked along the waterfront in the abandoned warehouse district. There was not an evil laugh to be heard.

No evil laughs? Some crime tsunami.

And then they heard something. Not an evil laugh—pieces of conversation. Something about

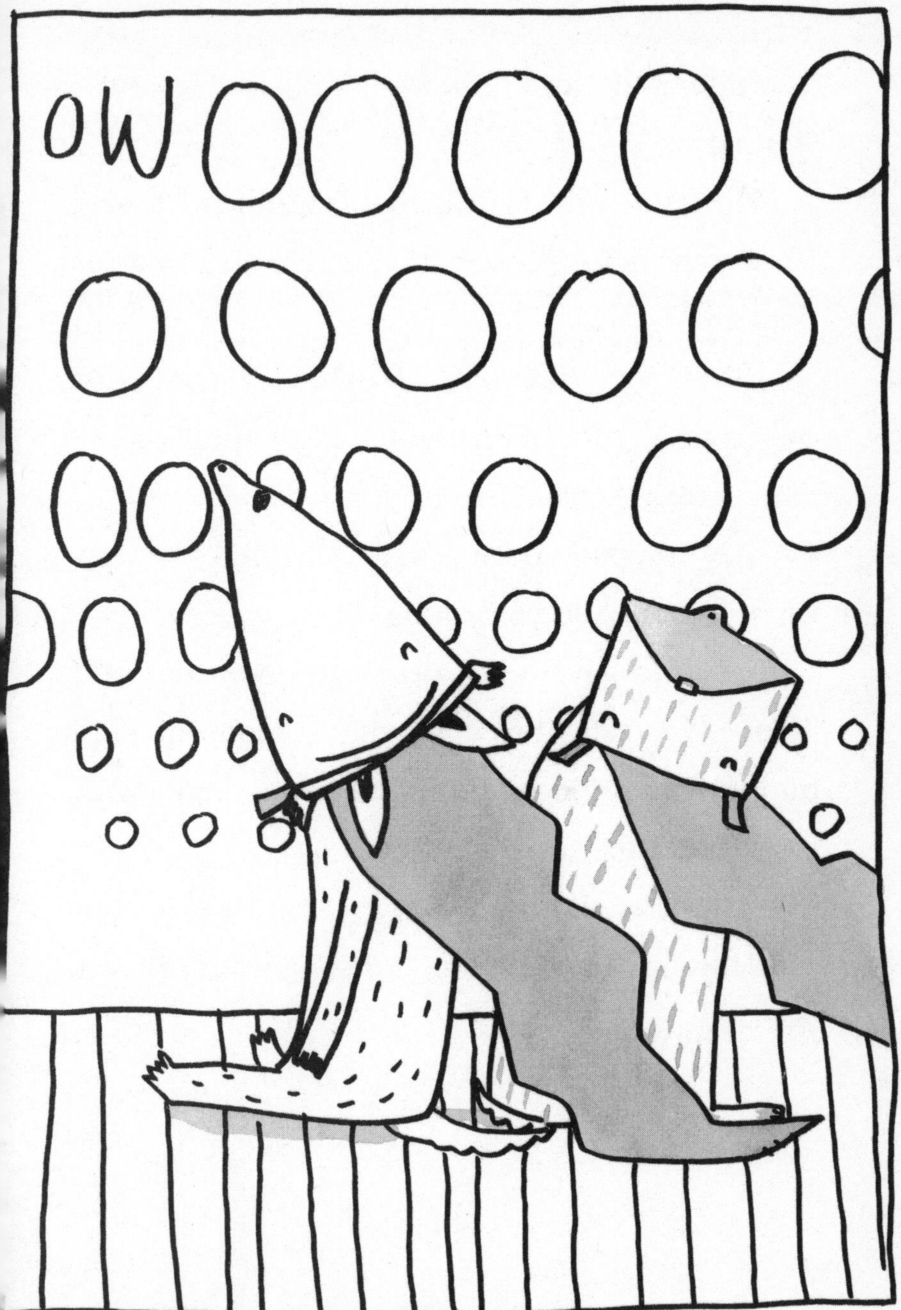
OW

a cruise ship and gazillionaires, jewels and a submarine.

"No wonder the evil laugh was muffled," Jo said. "You were right, Raymond. There is a submarine. Let's go."

"Go where?" Raymond's look said. They'd heard only pieces of conversation. They didn't know where it was coming from.

They stopped and listened. Nothing. But right then, Jo felt a sneeze coming on.

Raymond gave her a desperate look that said, "No!" He really loved having a moon-howling buddy. And someone to pee on fire hydrants with, for that matter.

But there was no stopping the sneeze, and suddenly Jo Schmo was no longer a werewolf. She was—

14

Boxing Skills

How do you keep the reader in suspense for an entire chapter? You'll have to wait until the next chapter to find out.

Numb Skull was so upset about Frankenstein's monster, who was currently taking a bite out of crime, that he didn't know what to do. Maybe go for a drive, he thought . . . in his submarine. And so while Harry Knuckles was cracking his knuckles and dreaming about punching security guards, and while Dyno-Mike was putting the finishing touches on a bomb big enough to sink a cruise ship, Numb Skull went for a spin in his submarine.

He submerged and made a few laps around San Francisco Bay, and as he did, he asked himself, "Why does this submarine have screen doors?"

That's what you call a design flaw.

He also thought of the jewel heist of the century. Or at least of the week. It wasn't going to be easy with Frankenstein's monster snooping around.

But Numb Skull was not the only one pondering his troubles that night beneath the surface of the bay.

Two hammerhead sharks named Phil and Harvey were swimming along, minding their own business, when they spotted something. "Would you look at that?" Phil said. "Just when you think you're the king of the bay."

"What is it?" Harvey said.

"Who cares? It's bigger than us."

"It looks like a gigantic metal hot dog."

"Good point." Phil loved hot dogs. Hot dogs were better than sea lions any day. "And there's two of us and only one of him."

Maybe they were the kings of the bay after all.

"Let's get him," Harvey said.

"Yes, let's," Phil agreed. They didn't have any ketchup or mustard, but no matter. Sometimes you just have to eat your hot dogs plain.

And so, with a swish of their fins, they took off. Actually, they swam, but you get the idea. The point is, they had always been kings, and they weren't going to let a gigantic metal hot dog stand in their way.

Numb Skull sat in his submarine and said, "Hmm . . ." As you know, saying "Hmm" meant something was wrong. And two hammerhead sharks, baring their teeth and swimming right at him, seemed, well . . . wrong. Not to mention scary.

Fortunately, the submarine was equipped with mechanical arms. He would use the arms to grab the jewels once Dyno-Mike sank the cruise ship full of gazillionaires. But they might come in handy to fight off a couple of hammerhead sharks.

Numb Skull grabbed the controls and got ready. "Mechanical Knuckle Sandwich coming right up," he said.

Each arm had a mechanical hand on the end. Numb Skull balled them into fists and—

Left cross!

Uppercut!

Phil and Harvey didn't know what hit them. But they sure felt it.

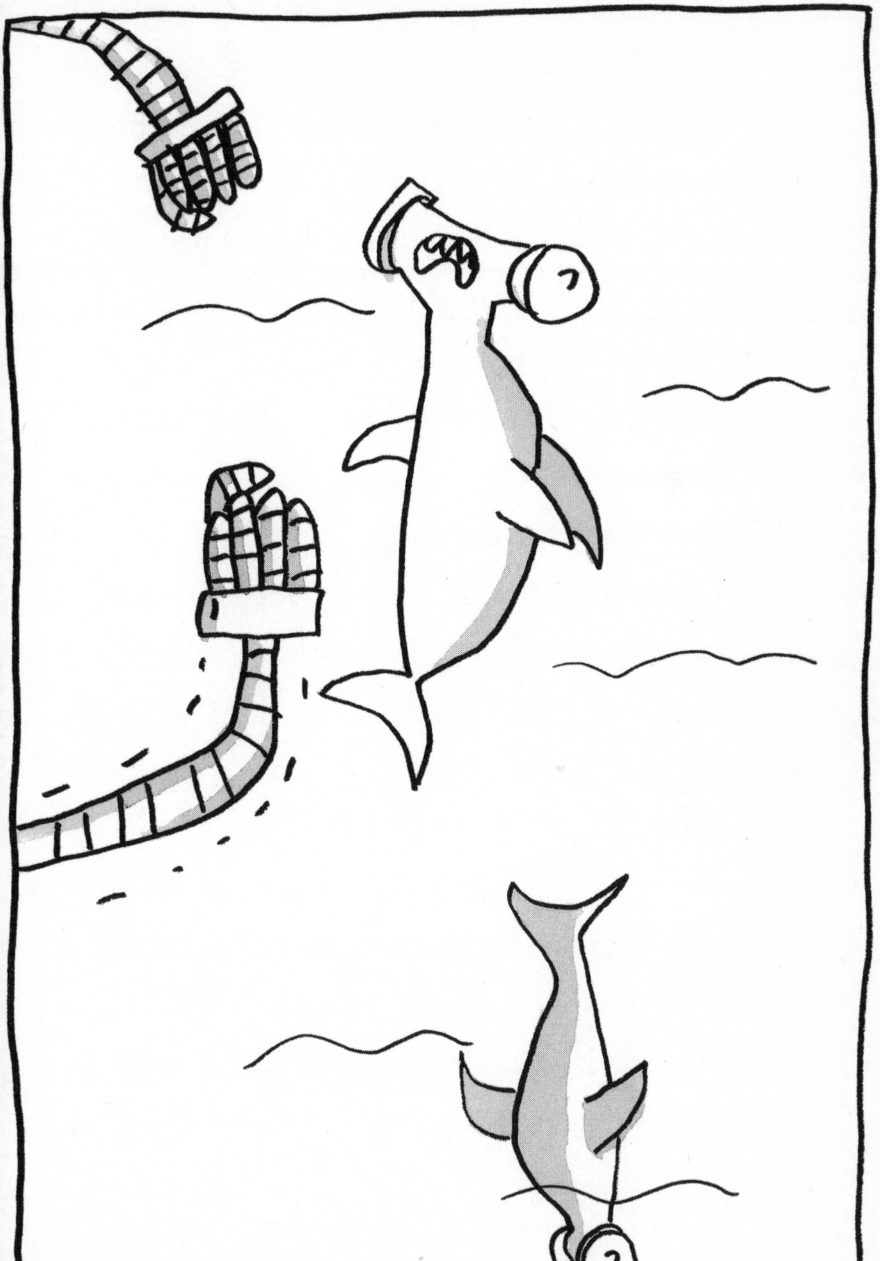

"I can't believe it," Phil said, rubbing his jaw with his fin. "A hot dog that knows how to box."

"Tell me about it."

But they weren't giving up so easily. They circled and came back for round two.

Round two was more of the same.

Right hook!

Body punch!

There wasn't a round three.

"I really didn't want a hot dog for dinner, anyway," said Phil.

"Me neither," said Harvey. "Let's go get some sea lion."

"Yes, let's," said Phil.

Moments later, Jo Schmo, who had just shape-shifted into a ———, heard a muffled *"Mwah-ha-ha!"* Someone inside a submarine was celebrating.

Goose Bumps

When Jo Schmo had sneezed she shape-shifted back into Mrs. Freep. Raymond gave her a look that said, "You again."

They wandered out of the abandoned warehouse district to the first diner they came to, a place called Margie's, and went inside. Actually, Jo went inside. Raymond stayed out. He might have been a superhero, but he was also a dog, and there were rules.

Jo walked up to a man who was typing on his

laptop. Using her best teacher voice—she was, after all, Mrs. Freep—she said, "Young man, may I use your computer for a few seconds? It's an emergency."

Jasper "Scoop" Johnson looked up at her. "Emergency?"

"Yes," Jo Schmo/Mrs. Freep said. "It involves saving human lives." It also involved cruise ships and jewels and muffled evil laughs, but she didn't have time to explain.

Jasper broke out in goose bumps. Saving human lives sounded a lot like a story. And Jasper "Scoop" Johnson was all about the story.

He let the lady with the teacher voice use his laptop, and he looked over her shoulder as she typed "cruise ship jewels gazillionaires San Francisco" into Google.

"Thanks!" she said a moment later as she ran for the door.

Once outside, she hopped on the Schmomobile, and she and Raymond raced toward the waterfront.

Raymond gave her a look that said, "You found something?"

"There's a cruise ship full of gazillionaires leaving tonight."

"And where you find gazillionaires you find jewels," Raymond's look said.

"And where you find jewels you find bad guys trying to steal them."

And where you find bad guys you find Jo Schmo and her Knuckle Sandwich.

But as they raced along, Jo wondered what all this had to do with a submarine. She looked down at Raymond and said, "A cruise ship is on top of the water and a submarine is under the water."

Raymond didn't say anything. He was too busy drooling, and it was difficult to drool and think at the same time.

When they reached the waterfront, they discovered another problem. There was more than one cruise ship. "Which one is it?" Jo asked.

Raymond pointed across the bay.

A ship was heading out to sea. People were wandering around the deck, and they were glittering in the moonlight.

"Diamonds," Jo said.

"Gazillionaires," Raymond's look said.

Hmm, Jo thought. *A ship full of gazillionaires.*

A submarine lurking beneath. She walked up and back on the dock, thinking. And then it hit her—

"They're going to sink the ship!" she said. "That's why they have a submarine."

The problem was that the ship was out there, and Jo and Raymond were still onshore. And Jo Schmo didn't know how to swim. I know . . . what kind of superhero doesn't know how to swim? She looked down at her dog and said, "It's up to you, Raymond. Can you get me to the ship?"

"Do dogs have fleas?" Raymond's look said. "Hang on."

Jo attached a leash to Raymond's collar. Then they jumped into the water and Raymond started dog-paddling. But this was not your average dog paddle. This was superhero dog paddle—zero to sixty in one minute and six seconds. As Raymond paddled, Jo hung on to the leash and water-skied behind him.

Water shot up from her feet into her nose, causing her to sneeze, and when she did, she shape-shifted.

But she didn't shift into Frankenstein's monster.

She didn't shift into a werewolf.

She didn't shift back into Jo Schmo.

She shifted into a ship's anchor and sank to the bottom of the bay. Unfortunately, anchors don't have noses. She couldn't sneeze herself into a different shape. She just sat at the bottom of the San Francisco Bay, looking very anchorlike.

16

Shifty Business

Raymond didn't realize that Jo had shape-shifted again and was now sitting at the bottom of the bay. But he did feel her let go of the leash. When he turned around, there was no sign of her.

His look said, "Where'd you go, Jo?"

There was only one place she could have gone. Down. And Raymond knew that Jo couldn't swim. He dove beneath the surface and looked around. There was nothing down there, just an anchor, looking very anchorlike.

It's me, Raymond, Jo thought. For some reason, the anchor had eyes. She could see Raymond dog-paddling above her. But she didn't have arms to move or a mouth that she could blow bubbles with. Or a nose to sneeze herself into another shape.

Things were looking pretty grim for Jo Schmo.

When Jasper "Scoop" Johnson heard the lady with the teacher voice say the word "emergency" and that it involved saving lives, he knew there was a story behind it. So he followed her and her dog as they raced toward the waterfront. For some reason, he found himself chasing people on motorized skateboards lately. Just the other day he had followed Frankenstein's monster. Chasing a lady with a teacher voice was much less scary.

Now he was standing on the dock, watching her water-ski behind a dog-paddling dog. And then, suddenly, she was gone.

What just happened? he thought. Were his eyes playing tricks on him? Did the teacher-voice lady just turn into an anchor and sink? No one would believe that story.

And right then, Jasper "Scoop" Johnson decided to quit the newspaper business and start writing fantasy stories for kids. It was way more interesting.

While Jasper "Scoop" Johnson was pondering a career change, Jo Schmo was sitting at the bottom of the bay, wondering what to do.

She thought back to the day her grandpa had read the chapter on shape-shifting. According to the manual, shape-shifting was all about thinking the right shape-shifting thoughts. Now, without arms, mouth, or nose, all she *had* were thoughts. She tried to clear her mind. All thoughts of home or school or friends or her mother's sponge cake— she put them aside. She even stopped thinking of Kevin with his great hair, Mitch, who looked spectacular in green, and David, with his seventeen adorable freckles.

It was now or never, either shape-shift or spend the rest of her life rusting away in the salt water. She put all her energy into shape-shifting. But she didn't want to change into Jo Schmo. She was at the bottom of the bay, and Jo Schmo couldn't swim.

Concentrate, she said to herself. *Shift into something that can swim.*

And before you could say "Jo Schmo shape-shifted into a killer whale and swam to the surface for a breath of fresh air," Jo Schmo shape-shifted into a killer whale and swam to the surface for a breath of fresh air.

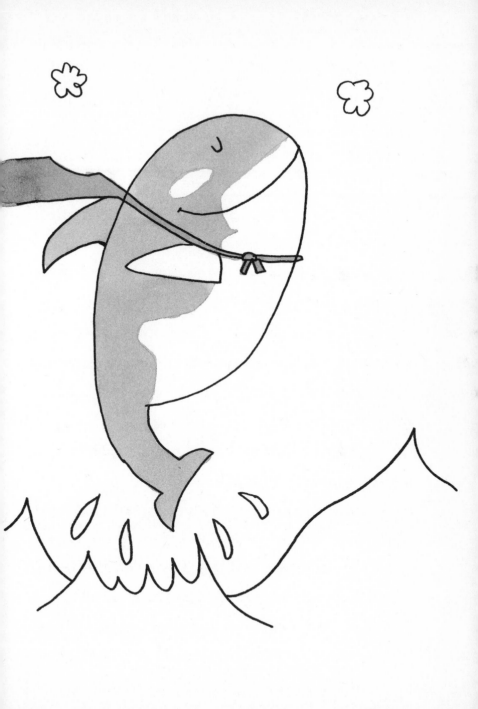

17

Whale of a Problem

Ever since the two hammerhead sharks, Phil and Harvey, had been punched in the nose by a gigantic metal hot dog, they'd been feeling pretty low.

"Would you look at that?" Phil said, pointing to a killer whale swimming to the surface for a breath of fresh air. "Just when you think you're the king of the bay."

Harvey nodded. "Tell me about it." The killer whale was even bigger than the hot dog.

And right then the two of them decided to leave

San Francisco Bay, and they were never seen in the area again. They moved to Mexico, where they had heard there weren't any killer whales.

The question was, were there any hot dogs with great boxing skills?

Raymond took one look at the killer whale and dog-paddled in the other direction. He didn't like the way the whale was looking at him. And he didn't like those teeth.

"It's me, Raymond. It's Jo."

Raymond kept paddling. Whales couldn't be trusted, especially ones who could talk.

"Raymond's the coolest dog ever."

Raymond stopped paddling and turned around. He gave her a look that said, "Wow. You've really put on weight, Jo."

Jo didn't have time to explain that she'd been an anchor for the past several minutes. There was no time. Someone was about to sink a cruise ship full of gazillionaires.

"Follow me," she said. She grabbed Raymond's leash in her teeth and swam as fast as her little fins could take her. Actually, they were big fins, but you get the idea.

When they reached the ship, Jo shape-shifted back into Jo Schmo. By now she'd gotten the hang of shape-shifting. It really was all about thinking the right shape-shifting thoughts. And she couldn't remain a killer whale if she wanted to get to the bottom of things. So she was back to her normal self. It felt good to have legs again.

Raymond gave her a look that said, "I missed you, boss."

"Thanks," Jo said. Then she grabbed Raymond and tossed him onto the deck of the ship and climbed up after him.

"Follow me, Raymond," Jo said as she ran along the deck.

"What are we looking for?" Raymond's look said.

"A bomb big enough to sink a cruise ship."

All the gazillionaires were inside having dinner. The decks were deserted, except for a few unconscious crew members, obviously the victims of someone's knuckle sandwich. Jo kept running. And this is what she saw:

Lounge chair, lounge chair, unconscious crew member, lounge chair, lounge chair, big box going *tick, tick, tick,* lounge chair, lounge chair—

Wait a second!

Jo stopped and backed up. There was a huge box with a digital clock attached, counting down the seconds.

30, 29, 28 . . .

Less than thirty seconds, Jo thought. She lifted the top off the bomb. The insides were full of whirling

gizmos and wires of different colors—red, blue, green, black.

One of them would deactivate the bomb. But choose the wrong one and *KABOOM!*

Jo was pretty sure that blowing herself up could ruin her whole day.

25, 24, 23 . . .

She started to sweat. "I built the Schmomobile," she told herself. "I created a time machine. I should be able to deactivate this thing."

But time was slipping away.

19, 18, 17 . . . tick, tick, tick . . .

18

KABOOM!

12, 11, 10 . . .

Jo looked at the red, blue, black, and green wires. Which one was it?

Raymond's look said, "Don't look at me. I'm just a dog."

7, 6, 5 . . .

"Red," Jo said. "It's gotta be the red one. Red is the color of fireworks. It's the color of things that go *KERPOW.*"

Not to mention *KABOOM.*

Jo reached for the red wire, but Raymond put out a paw to stop her. Then he gave her a look that said, "Isn't that an ON/OFF switch?" Raymond didn't know how to read, but he was pretty sure he'd seen those words before.

Jo flipped the switch, and the ticking stopped.

Just in the elbow of time.

Oops!

Just in the nick of time.

"Good work, Raymond," Jo said.

"Thank you," Raymond's look said.

Now that the bomb was deactivated, Jo picked it up and tossed it out to sea.

KABOOM!

Guess it wasn't deactivated after all.

The explosion didn't sink the ship, but it did cause a large metal hot dog to surface. Seconds later a hatch on top opened and out poured smoke, followed by Numb Skull, Harry Knuckles, and Dyno-Mike.

The first thing out of Numb Skull's mouth was, "Curses!" followed by . . . some curses.

Raymond's look said, "Perpetrators!" which is dog language for bad guys.

And right then Jo sneezed.

Raymond couldn't bear to look at her. Who knew what he'd find? Frankenstein's monster? A werewolf? Mrs. Freep? A killer whale?

AAqq-Choooo!!

But it was just Jo. She was still one hundred percent Jo Schmo. Not only could she shape-shift when she wanted to by thinking the right shape-shifting thoughts, she could also *not* shift when she sneezed.

Numb Skull and company were still standing on top of the submarine, coughing from all the smoke.

"Sponge cake!" Jo yelled. This was the lofty thought that caused her to fly. She swooped down on the trio of bad guys. "Knuckle Sandwiches coming right up." Numb Skull, Harry Knuckles, and Dyno-Mike didn't know what hit them. But they sure felt it.

Jo and Raymond hung around until the Coast Guard arrived to haul the bad guys off to jail, then she and Raymond took off. Literally.

"Sponge cake," she said, lifting off the ground, holding Raymond.

The gazillionaires, who had heard the explosion and were now standing on the deck, cheered. It was nice to have a superhero in town.

Moments later, Jo and Raymond touched down lightly in their backyard on Crimshaw Avenue and went in to talk to Grandpa Joe. He'd heard all about it on the police radio. He'd even heard the *KABOOM*.

"Great work, Jo," he said. He loved having a

granddaughter who saved the world. Not to mention cruise ships.

Once word got around that Numb Skull's evil plan had failed, the crime tsunami all but died away. It went from crime tsunami to crime wave to crime ripple to calm seas.

"It's all because of you, Jo," Grandpa Joe said proudly. "How do you feel?"

"It wasn't all me, Gramps," Jo said, looking down at her dog. "I had help. How do you feel, Raymond?"

Raymond gave her a look that said, "Not too shabby." Then he gave her another look that said, "We should celebrate."

"Excellent," Grandpa Joe said. "What should we do?"

Jo smiled. She knew the perfect way to celebrate. On Friday afternoon, after she got home from school, she shape-shifted into a frog, hopped into her grandpa's shirt pocket, and, for the first time in her life, got into the movies for free.